PUFFIN BOOKS

The Ghost at No. 13

Hamlet Orlando Julius Caesar Brown has a problem —
and it's not his name. It's his sister Susan. There's
nothing wrong with Susan; in fact she's perfect in
every way — and that's the problem because having
someone as special as Susan as your older sister makes
you feel very ordinary indeed! And even though
everyone likes Susan, most days Hamlet loathes her (and
some days he even *hates* her) because he cannot stand
goodie-goodies and having such a good goodie-goodie
as Susan as your sister can be very difficult indeed.

But then one night, after a visit to the fair, something
quite extraordinary happens to Hamlet for a change,
which makes him feel that he's not so ordinary after all.

Gyles Brandreth is the author of many books of
quizzes, puzzles, games and jokes. He is also a well-
known children's television personality. He lives in
London with his wife and three children.

GYLES BRANDRETH

The Ghost at No. 13

Illustrated by Julie Tennent

PUFFIN BOOKS

To Michèle

PUFFIN BOOKS

Published by the Penguin Group
27 Wrights Lane, London W8 5TZ, England
Viking Penguin Inc., 40 West 23rd Street, New York, New York 10010, USA
Penguin Books Australia Ltd, Ringwood, Victoria, Australia
Penguin Books Canada Ltd, 2801 John Street, Markham, Ontario, Canada L3R 1B4
Penguin Books (NZ) Ltd, 182–190 Wairau Road, Auckland 10, New Zealand

Penguin Books Ltd, Registered Offices: Harmondsworth, Middlesex, England

First published by Viking Kestrel 1985
Published in Puffin Books 1987
10 9 8

Made and printed in Great Britain by
Richard Clay Ltd, Bungay, Suffolk
Filmset in Monophoto Palatino

1. A Boy Called Hamlet

Hamlet Orlando Julius Caesar Brown had a problem. And it wasn't his name. It was his sister Susan.

Hamlet was nine years old and lived at No. 13 Irving Terrace, Hammersmith, West London. Hamlet felt that No. 13 was a very unlucky house at which to live because Susan lived there too and Hamlet considered himself the unluckiest boy in the world because he had Susan as a sister.

There was nothing wrong with Susan. That was the problem. Susan was perfect. She was only eleven but everybody said she was the cleverest eleven-year-old they had ever met,

and Mrs Norgate – the head teacher – said she was much cleverer than most twelve-year-olds as well.

At school Susan was always top of the class and she was the teachers' favourite because she behaved so nicely. 'She has perfect

manners,' said Mrs Norgate, 'and a perfectly sweet smile.' Hamlet thought Susan's smile was a sickly grin – and it made his stomach turn just to see it – but then Hamlet wasn't a goodie-goodie and he didn't like goodie-goodies and he considered Susan to be the goodiest goodie-goodie he had ever come across.

Not that Hamlet was an especially naughty boy. He didn't tell lies, unless you call saying you've washed your hands when you haven't a lie. And he didn't have any very bad habits, unless you count picking your nose as a very bad habit. And he wasn't an especially stupid boy. He was never top of the class, but he was never bottom of the class either. He was just ordinary. In fact he was about as ordinary as you can get. The only special thing about him was his name.

Hamlet's father was an actor, which is how Hamlet came to be called Hamlet Orlando Julius Caesar Brown. They were the names of three of the characters Mr Brown had played in the year that Hamlet was born. Susan was called Susan because Mr Brown was out of work in the year she was born and because Mrs Brown liked the name. It was her sister's name and Mrs Brown liked her sister.

Hamlet wanted to like *his* sister (he did, he really did), but it can be difficult to like someone who is supposed to be so very special when you know you're so very ordinary. Some days Hamlet almost managed to like his sister. Most days he loathed her. Today he *hated* her, but then today was the last day of the summer term and Hamlet and Susan had both come home from school bringing their end-of-term reports with them.

Mr Brown was sitting at the head of the kitchen table drinking a mug of tea when Mrs Brown came in with the children. 'Ah, my young cubs have returned!' said Mr Brown dramatically. 'And what, oh what, have they brought with them?'

'Their school reports, of course,' said Mrs Brown rather crossly.

Mrs Brown was an actress, but she still

thought Mr Brown was rather silly to talk as
if he was acting in a play when he was really
sitting in the kitchen having a mug of tea.

'Do not be cross with me, fair wife,' said
Mr Brown, pouring her out some tea. 'It is
just my way.'

And so it was. Wherever he was, whatever
he was doing, Mr Brown *always* talked as if
he was on a stage in a theatre acting a very

dramatic part in a very exciting play. 'How is't with you, fair daughter of mine?' he would say to Susan when all he meant was 'How are you?' And 'Prince Hamlet, what hour o' the clock hast thou?' was his way of asking his son the time.

Even though Mrs Brown found her husband's manner of speaking rather irritating, Susan and Hamlet quite liked it. There were embarrassing moments — like the time Mr Brown made the postman kneel down to be knighted with the bread knife because he'd brought a letter containing some money that Mr Brown had been waiting for for weeks — but on the whole the children were amused by their father's funny theatrical ways.

'Now, my children, let me see these reports,' said Mr Brown, and Hamlet and Susan handed over their reports so that their father could read them out loud. 'I am sure they will be wonderful as usual.'

Hamlet was sure that Susan's would be wonderful as usual. And so it was. Once again Susan was top of the class in every single subject and Mrs Norgate declared that 'Susan Brown is a real credit to her school. She is an exceptional child and it is a pleasure teaching her.'

When Mr Brown had finished reading out Susan's report — and to Hamlet it seemed to take forever — Mrs Brown kissed her daughter and Mr Brown said, 'Well done, my child!'

Susan smiled sweetly. Hamlet felt sick.

'And now,' continued Mr Brown in his booming actor's voice, 'let us hear what the school has to say about young Hamlet.'

And Mr Brown began to read out Hamlet's report. It wasn't as bad as it might have been. None of it was terrible and some bits were quite good. It was sort of average, and if it hadn't been for the fact that Susan's report was so incredibly wonderful everybody would probably have thought Hamlet's report was really very good.

'Not at all bad, my son,' said Mr Brown when he had finished reading it out. Mrs Brown kissed Hamlet. Hamlet made a face.

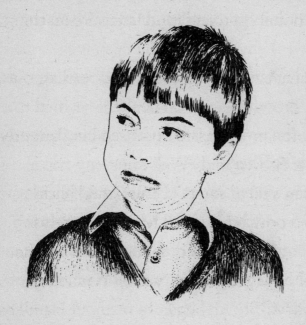

'There's no need to pull silly faces,' said Mrs Brown. 'At least you can forget all about school till next term.'

'No I can't,' said Hamlet with a groan. 'We've got to do a beastly holiday project.'

'Yes,' said Susan enthusiastically. 'We can all choose our own subject and there are going to be prizes for the best project in each class.'

'And we all know who's going to win the prize in your class,' sneered Hamlet, who hated doing projects and hated Susan for loving them and doing them so well.

'That's no way to speak to your sister,' said Mrs Brown.

'I don't mind,' said Susan, smiling sweetly at her brother.

'Say you're sorry, Hamlet,' said his mother.

'Sorry!' said Hamlet, who only felt sorry for himself. 'It's just that I don't think it's much of a holiday if you've got to do school work during it.'

'I think the project's going to be great fun,' said Susan happily. 'I'm going to start as soon as I've done my piano practice.'

And with that she left the room. Hamlet followed her out, and when he was sure his

parents couldn't see him he stuck his tongue
out at his sister. Then, feeling a little better,
he went to see what was on TV.

2. Friday the Thirteenth

The next day was Friday — Friday the thirteenth, as a matter of fact — and Hamlet was sure it was going to be another unlucky day at No. 13 Irving Terrace.

It began badly with boiled eggs for breakfast. Hamlet hated boiled eggs. He could just about swallow the yellow part, but the white bit made him feel sick. Susan, of course, loved boiled eggs and enjoyed the white part — which, naturally, she knew was correctly called the albumen — just as much as the yolk. From Hamlet's point of view the only good thing about a boiled egg was that when you had finished it you could turn it

upside down in the eggcup and beat its head in!

After breakfast both Mr and Mrs Brown went out to work. Mrs Brown didn't work very often, but when she did she earned a lot of money — much more than Mr Brown — because Mrs Brown's speciality as an actress was recording the voices that go with television commercials. She only recorded about one of these 'voice-overs' as she called them every six weeks or so and the recording session never lasted more than an hour, but Mrs Brown earned hundreds and hundreds of pounds from this work because she got paid every single time the advertisement using her voice was shown on TV.

Mrs Brown was looking forward to today's recording because although she was only going to record seven words, those seven words were going to help advertise a new brand of toothpaste and Mrs Brown knew that her voice encouraging everyone to 'Buy Ultradent for the brightest whitest smile' would soon be heard coming out of millions of television sets night after night for weeks and months — and maybe even years — to come.

Mr Brown was in a good mood too because although he wasn't going to be earning a lot of money that day he was going to be doing what he loved doing best: rehearsing a new play. In fact, the play he was rehearsing was a very old play – almost four hundred years old – but it was a new production of the old play and it was Mr Brown's favourite play written by Mr Brown's favourite playwright, William Shakespeare.

The play was called *Hamlet* and Mr Brown had last acted in it in the year that his son was born. That was nine years ago, of course, when Mr Brown had played the main part of Hamlet himself. This time he was playing the much smaller part of Hamlet's father.

To be honest, Mr Brown was a little offended not to have been asked to play the main part again, especially as the actor who was playing the part this time wasn't very good. At least, according to Mr Brown he wasn't.

'He's so bad,' Mr Brown had told the family

at breakfast, 'that I won't be surprised if the audience throw eggs at him on the first night.'

'If they do,' said Mrs Brown, 'he'll go on as Hamlet and come off as omelette!'

Mr and Mrs Brown laughed a lot at this joke, which just shows what a good mood they were in.

Susan was in a good mood too. As soon as her parents had set off for work, she set about clearing the kitchen table. Then she got out her notebooks and her pens and pencils and all the bits and pieces she needed for her project and laid them neatly in front of her.

'My project's going to be all about the human body,' she said to Hamlet, who was looking at the newspaper to see if there was anything to watch on TV. 'What's your project going to be about?'

'I don't know,' said Hamlet grumpily. There was nothing to watch on the box. Hamlet only really liked cartoons and old black and white comedies and there weren't any of those on till the afternoon.

'The human body is fascinating,' said Susan

brightly. 'Did you know that the average adult skeleton contains 206 bones?'

'No, I didn't,' said Hamlet with a scowl.

'And don't you think it's amazing that you can make seven bars of soap with the fat in one human body?'

'No, I don't,' said Hamlet, who was looking and feeling pretty miserable.

'It must be hard work looking so gloomy,' said his sister. 'You know it takes forty-three

muscles to frown, but only seventeen to smile.'

'Oh do shut up, Susan!' said Hamlet, frowning furiously.

'Why are you so fed up?'

'You'd be fed up if you couldn't think what to do for your project, wouldn't you?'

'Why don't you do dinosaurs?' Susan was trying to be helpful now. 'If I hadn't decided to do the human body,' she said, 'I'd have done dinosaurs. They're fascinating.'

Hamlet — who couldn't tell the difference between a Diplodocus and a Tyrannosaurus Rex and certainly couldn't spell either — didn't think much of his sister's suggestion.

'If you did dinosaurs I could help you,' said Susan.

Hamlet thought that was positively the worst idea he'd ever heard. 'No thanks,' he said, and he hurried out of the kitchen before Susan could make any more crazy suggestions.

He went to his room and lay down on his bed and gazed at the ceiling. 'I'm bored,' he thought to himself. And he was.

3. All the Fun of the Fair

Saturday was a lot better than Friday.
Saturday at No. 13 Irving Terrace was
always a bit special because on Saturday
morning Mr Brown gave everyone breakfast
in bed.

He got up early and went to the kitchen on
his own where he put on a stripey apron and
a chef's hat – Mr Brown *loved* dressing up –
and then spent about an hour making an awful
lot of noise and quite a lot of mess preparing
what was really a very simple meal: tea for
himself, coffee for Mrs Brown, orange juice
for the children, and toast and honey for
everybody.

When he had finished preparing the breakfast he laid it all out on a huge tray and carried it upstairs to his bedroom.

Mrs Brown was still in bed and fast asleep. Recording the seven words of the toothpaste commercial on Friday had exhausted her. In any event, she never woke up when Mr Brown was making breakfast, because in bed she always wore special earplugs to keep out the noise. She also wore an eyeshade to keep out the light, so she slept very soundly.

On Saturday mornings as a special treat Hamlet and Susan were allowed into their parents' bedroom for breakfast. They sat at the end of the bed and it was their arrival that woke up Mrs Brown who was sometimes a little grumpy first thing in the morning.

Mr Brown was usually rather cheerful on Saturday mornings and this seemed to make Mrs Brown even grumpier. Mr Brown was cheerful because he felt specially pleased with himself whenever he made breakfast for the family.

Today he felt particularly cheerful because yesterday's rehearsals had gone extremely well. The actor Mr Brown didn't like – the one playing the main part – was having a lot of difficulty remembering his lines, while Mr Brown knew all of his.

'Good morning, sweet children,' he said to Hamlet and Susan as he handed them their orange juice and toast. 'Prithee, no crumbs in the bed now!'

At one end of the bed Hamlet and Susan tucked into their breakfast while at the other end Mrs Brown was slowly waking up. When she had taken out her earplugs and removed her eyeshade Mr Brown greeted her with the words 'Hail to thee blithe spirit,' and handed her a cup of coffee. At the same time he bent over to kiss her on the forehead and managed to spill the coffee all over the place.

'Oh, forgive me, dearest wife!' cried Mr Brown.

'Only if you stop talking in that ridiculous way,' said Mrs Brown crossly. 'It gets on my nerves.'

Mr Brown muttered 'Sorry dear' and did his best to mop up the mess with his apron.

'It's no use trying to mop it up,' said Mrs Brown. 'Coffee stains won't come out. The sheet's ruined. We'll have to throw it out.'

'Oh dear,' said Mr Brown, who was feeling very guilty now.

'Oh dear,' said Susan from her end of the bed.

Hamlet decided not to say anything. In fact it was all he could do to stop himself from giggling. Whenever his mother told his father off – and she did it quite often – it made Hamlet want to giggle. Mrs Brown caught sight of him now.

'And what's so funny, may I ask?'

'Nothing, Mum,' said Hamlet trying not to giggle.

'Then wipe that silly smirk off your face at once – or there'll be no end-of-term treat for you, young man.'

This was the first Hamlet had heard of any end-of-term treat, but it sounded interesting,

so he wiped the smirk off his face at once and inquired, 'What end-of-term treat, Mum?'

'While *I* change the sheet *and* make the bed *and* clear up the kitchen *and* get the lunch, your father is going to take you and your sister to Ealing Common.'

'To Ealing Common? What for?' asked Mr Brown, who was hearing about the end-of-term treat for the first time too.

'For the fun fair, of course!' said Mrs Brown, as if everybody should have known all about it. 'It's only on today and tomorrow so if you don't hurry up and get along there you'll find it's too crowded to enjoy. Off you go now! I can't have you cluttering up the place here. I've got work to do.'

So saying Mrs Brown went off to have a bath and Mr Brown, Hamlet and Susan got dressed as quickly as they could.

Mr Brown and Hamlet loved fun fairs. Susan thought they were a waste of time and money and she really wanted to stay at home and get on with her project, but she didn't say so.

The three of them arrived at Ealing Common by half past ten. It wasn't crowded at all and they spent two hours – and about five pounds – having the most marvellous time.

At least, Mr Brown and Hamlet had the most marvellous time. Susan didn't enjoy any of it much. She *quite* liked the old-fashioned merry-go-round, and she sort of enjoyed the shooting range because she managed to score a bull's eye and won a large pink teddy bear.

Mr Brown's favourites were the helter-skelter and a game where you threw a ball at a target and if you hit it a lady would fall out of bed! Susan thought it was a particularly silly game.

None of them really enjoyed the trip on the very fast rollercoaster called Wild Mouse

(even Mr Brown screamed), but Hamlet had a lot of fun on the dodgem cars — he managed to ram poor Susan's car eight times — and he fell about laughing in the hall of crazy mirrors. Susan didn't like being made to look longer and shorter and fatter and thinner than she really was, but Hamlet liked looking silly. He liked his sister looking silly too!

At half past twelve, Mr Brown looked at his watch and said, 'Time for just one more ride. What's it going to be?'

'The ghost train!' shouted Hamlet.

'Oh no, not the ghost train,' said Susan.

'You're just frightened,' said Hamlet.

'No I'm not,' said Susan. 'Not a bit.'

So they went on the ghost train and it *was* a bit frightening. As they rattled along dark tunnels they heard terrible screams and horrid ghostly green faces kept popping out at them. They hurtled past skeletons and vampires and a very fierce-looking dog with bright red eyes!

When they came out the other end Hamlet was jolly glad it was over.

'I didn't find it frightening at all,' said Susan.

She was telling the truth, but what she didn't tell her brother was that she hadn't really seen or heard anything on the ghost train. She had her eyes shut tight and her fingers in her ears throughout the ride.

'I thought it was frightening but fun,' said Hamlet.

'I thought it was very silly,' said Susan. 'Anyway I don't believe in ghosts.'

'Oh, I do,' said Hamlet.

'I do too,' said Mr Brown, very definitely.

'Well I don't,' said Susan.

'I also believe in lunch,' said Mr Brown, 'and if we don't go now we'll be late – and then we'll be in real trouble!'

4. The Night Visitor

When Hamlet went to bed that night he was feeling a lot happier than he had felt the night before. Saturday had been a much jollier day than Friday at No. 13 Irving Terrace. Hamlet had enjoyed going to the fun fair in the morning. And he had enjoyed watching the old black and white comedy on the television in the afternoon. And now it was night time and he was ready for bed.

Hamlet was feeling very tired and no sooner had he turned out his light and snuggled down into his bed than he fell fast asleep.

He would have stayed fast asleep till

breakfast if something hadn't woken him in
the middle of the night. It was a loud bang —
like a door slamming — and it woke Hamlet
up with a start. He sat up in bed and looked
at his luminous watch. It was exactly midnight.
Hamlet had never been awake at midnight

before. It felt very strange. To be honest, it felt rather spooky.

Hamlet looked around him but he couldn't see anything because it was so dark. He got out of bed and turned on the light. The light seemed very bright indeed, but the room looked just as it always did. Hamlet switched off the light again and scrambled back into bed. He snuggled right down, closed his eyes and tried to get back to sleep.

But Hamlet couldn't get back to sleep. The harder he tried the more wide awake he felt. And then he thought he heard another noise. Not a bang this time, more a sort of gentle rumbling – like a very, very quiet car engine or a very, very loud cat purring. The noise seemed to be coming from somewhere in the room.

Hamlet was quite frightened now. He jumped out of bed and as fast as he could he switched on the light. The room looked just as it always did.

Hamlet stood stock still and listened. He could still hear the gentle rumbling sound. It seemed to be coming from the corner of his bedroom. It seemed to be coming from inside the cupboard in the corner of his bedroom. It seemed to be getting louder.

Hamlet tiptoed slowly towards the cupboard. His heart was beating faster now, but Hamlet wasn't a coward. It was midnight and there was a strange noise coming from the cupboard in the corner of his bedroom and Hamlet was going to find out what it was.

He reached the cupboard and he counted to three – one, two, three – and he pulled open the cupboard door, and there it was – A GHOST!

Yes, sitting inside the cupboard, on the floor, fast asleep and snoring gently, there was a ghost.

Hamlet knew it was a ghost at once because it looked exactly like a ghost. It was all white and shaped like a floating sheet. It didn't seem to have any legs or arms, but it definitely had a head and two dark holes for eyes. It looked a friendly sort of ghost, but what on earth was it doing fast asleep on the floor of Hamlet's bedroom cupboard on a Saturday night in the middle of July?

And what on earth was Hamlet going to do about it?

He thought he'd better go for help. He didn't like the idea of asking Susan for advice, but she was his sister and she was two years older than him and she was in the next door room. So he closed the cupboard door and ran quickly and quietly into Susan's room.

He switched on Susan's bedside light and shook his sister gently.

'Susan, Susan,' he whispered, 'wake up.'

'What is it?' Susan said blearily, opening

her eyes and rubbing them. 'What's going on?'

'Come quickly,' said Hamlet. 'There's a ghost in my bedroom.'

'A *what*?' said Susan, who was half asleep and couldn't believe her ears.

'A ghost. There's a ghost in my bedroom,' said Hamlet.

'Don't be daft,' said his sister.

'But there is, I promise you – a real live ghost!'

'And what's he doing?' asked Susan scornfully.

'He's fast asleep on the floor in my cupboard.'

'Oh, don't be ridiculous, Hamlet. There are no such things as ghosts! Now go back to bed and let me get some sleep, will you?'

And Susan switched off her light and put her head under the pillow and that was that.

Hamlet tiptoed back to his own room. The

gentle snoring sound was still coming from the cupboard. Hamlet opened the cupboard door and the ghost was still sitting there, sleeping as peacefully as ever.

'So she thinks there are no such things as ghosts, does she?' Hamlet muttered to himself angrily. 'Well, I'll show her.' And he closed

the cupboard and marched straight back into his sister's bedroom and switched on her light.

'Susan!' he commanded. 'Susan!'

'What is it now?'

'Susan, there is a ghost in my bedroom and I want you to come and see it. And I want you to come and see it *now!*'

'Don't be such a silly billy. You've just had a bad dream, that's all. Now leave me alone and go back to bed.'

'I've not had a bad dream. I won't leave you alone. And I won't go back to bed. I am telling you there is a ghost in my bedroom and I want you to come and see it with your own eyes.'

And so saying he grabbed hold of his sister and dragged her out of bed.

'Oh all right, all right, I'm coming,' said Susan, pulling on her dressing gown and slippers.

Hamlet led the way back to his bedroom.

'Where's this ghost of yours then?' said Susan when she came into the room and found it looking the same as it always did.

'Over here,' whispered Hamlet, leading her to the cupboard in the corner. 'Now close your eyes and count to three and I'll open the cupboard door. Then we'll see who's the silly billy!'

Susan shut her eyes and counted to three: 'One – two – three!'

With a grand gesture, Hamlet pulled open the cupboard door – but there was nothing there. The ghost had gone and the cupboard was bare.

5. 'Welcome'

On Sunday morning it was Mrs Brown's turn to make breakfast, while Mr Brown had a lie-in. Hamlet usually liked Mrs Brown's Sunday morning breakfast because it was a big one and included all his favourites — bacon, baked beans, and mushrooms — but this Sunday he wasn't feeling very hungry.

'I don't think Hamlet's feeling very well today,' said Susan, in the superior voice she used when she wanted to annoy her brother.

Hamlet stuck his tongue out at Susan.

'Don't do that, Hamlet,' said his mother sharply.

'He can't help it, Mum,' said Susan looking

very serious. 'I think he's going round the bend.'

'Really Susan,' said Mrs Brown frowning at her daughter. 'What a thing to say!'

'It's true though. He's started seeing things – and that's a sure sign of madness, isn't it?'

Mrs Brown didn't know what to make of any of this. Hamlet stuck his tongue out at his sister again.

'He says he saw a ghost last night!' said Susan.

'Well I did!' said Hamlet.

'Well I never!' said Mrs Brown.

'I *did* see a ghost last night. I did. I did. I did!'

Hamlet was almost shouting now and Mrs Brown was looking quite worried.

'I'm sure it was only a bad dream, dear,' she said, 'nothing to worry about.'

'It was a ghost I tell you,' said Hamlet, 'and I'm not worried about it. There was a real live ghost in my bedroom last night and I don't care if you believe it or not.'

'Where's it gone now then?' asked Susan.

'I don't know,' said Hamlet.

'Now you two,' said Mrs Brown, 'stop quarrelling. Let's just finish our breakfast and then we can have a nice quiet day and forget all about it.'

But Hamlet couldn't forget all about it. After breakfast, while Susan went back to work on her project – and discovered that almost half the heat in your body is lost through the top of your head and that people with blonde hair have more hairs on their heads than people with brown hair – Hamlet went back up to his bedroom and started to clear out his cupboard. He took everything out of the cupboard – clothes, shoes, football boots, some rusty roller skates, a magic set he hardly ever used, a broken train set in an old cardboard box – and shoved it all underneath his bed.

When the cupboard was quite empty he dusted it, using his pyjama bottoms as a duster. When the cupboard was quite clean he set about making it as cosy and as comfortable as he could. He put a small rug

on the floor of the cupboard and his pillow on top of the rug. He sorted out his favourite comics and put them in the cupboard as well. Finally, he wrote the word WELCOME in large letters on a piece of paper and pinned the message to the inside of the cupboard door.

52

That night, when it was bedtime, Hamlet undressed, washed, brushed his teeth and got into bed as usual. But he didn't turn off his light and he didn't lie down. He sat up in bed and he waited. He waited and he waited and he waited.

And he waited.

And then he waited.

And then he waited some more.

He waited until midnight. Believe it or not, he waited until one o'clock. But nothing happened. He didn't hear a sound. Nobody came.

At breakfast the next morning, Susan asked him in her sweetest voice, 'Meet any ghosts last night?'

'No,' said Hamlet crossly, 'as a matter of fact I didn't. But even if I had met a ghost I wouldn't tell you.'

That night Hamlet waited for the ghost again, but because he had waited up so long

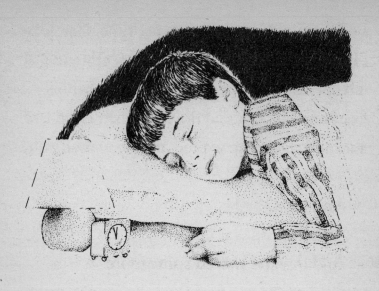

the night before, he was very, very tired and
he found it was very, very difficult to stay
awake. At about half past ten, with the light
still on, Hamlet fell fast asleep.

He slept soundly till midnight when
suddenly he woke up with a jump. What was
that? He'd heard a noise, a bang, a something.
He wasn't sure what it was, but it made him
leap up out of bed and run to the cupboard in
the corner. He flung open the cupboard door
and there – yes, right there in Hamlet Brown's

bedroom at No. 13 Irving Terrace, Hammersmith, West London – was a ghost, sitting on Hamlet's rug, leaning against Hamlet's pillow, reading Hamlet's 'Welcome' note.

'How do you do,' said the ghost in a friendly whisper.

'How do you do,' said Hamlet very quietly.

'Thank you for making me so welcome,' said the ghost.

'Not at all,' said Hamlet.

The ghost looked up at Hamlet and seemed to smile.

'By the way, I'm Hamlet,' said Hamlet, feeling it was about time he introduced himself.

'And I'm a ghost,' said the ghost, giving a little bow.

'It's nice to meet you,' said Hamlet.

'And it's nice to meet you,' said the ghost. And he sounded as if he meant it.

'If you don't think it's rude my asking,' said Hamlet, 'what are you doing here?'

'I'm afraid I'm lost,' said the ghost sadly. 'Hopelessly lost.'

'Oh dear,' said Hamlet, not quite knowing what else he could say.

'You see I'm on holiday,' explained the ghost. 'It's my first holiday in five hundred years. I've been looking forward to it for ages – for centuries in fact – but it hasn't turned out at all as I'd expected.'

'Where have you come from?' said Hamlet.

'Denmark,' said the ghost. 'Do you know it?'

'I'm afraid not,' said Hamlet, who had only been abroad once and that was on a day trip to France.

'It's a lovely country, Denmark,' said the ghost. 'You should go.'

'I will, I promise,' said Hamlet quickly, not having the first idea how he was ever going to get to go to Denmark but feeling that he must do his best to make polite conversation with his new friend.

'I should never have left home,' continued the ghost. 'It was a great mistake. But it's not every day you get two months' holiday and I didn't want to stay at a ghost-house by the sea like all the others do. I wanted a bit of adventure. I wanted to see the world. I wanted to explore the happy haunting grounds beyond the sea ...'

'So you're here for a holiday?' said Hamlet.

'Yes, that's the general idea,' said the ghost, 'but I didn't realize that Great Britain would be so much bigger than Denmark. And I haven't got anywhere to stay. And I haven't got a map. And I'm lost and alone and –'

Hamlet thought the poor ghost was about to burst into tears. 'Please don't be sad,' he said. 'You can stay here if you like.'

'Oh can I?' said the ghost, brightening up

at once. 'Can I really? I won't be in your way, will I?'

'Not at all,' said Hamlet, who was delighted at the idea of having a house-ghost for the summer. 'You can stay for as long as you like.'

'I can only stay for two months,' said the ghost. 'Then I have to get back to Elsinore. That's where I live. I work there too, of course. I've got my own castle you know. It's very big. You must come and see it some day.'

'I will,' said Hamlet, who knew at once that he would feel very much at home at Elsinore Castle.

'Of course we've got castles in Britain too,' he added.

'I know,' said the ghost, 'and I want to visit them all while I'm here. Have you got a map?'

Hamlet went over to his bookshelf and got out his atlas. He had always thought an atlas was a very boring sort of book — till now. Hamlet's atlas turned out to be *exactly* the kind of atlas they needed. It contained a very useful road map of the whole country and an even more useful map called 'Historic Britain' which showed you where to find all the most famous castles and old buildings in the land.

'This is splendid,' said the ghost. 'I can go out sightseeing every day and come back here every night. Perhaps I should start by visiting the Tower of London in the morning. What do you think?'

'I think that's a very good idea,' said Hamlet, who had been to the Tower of London twice and enjoyed his visits greatly.

The ghost chuckled with pleasure. 'I can tell I'm going to have the most marvellous holiday after all,' he said.

'So am I,' said Hamlet, grinning from ear to ear.

And the friendly ghost winked at Hamlet and Hamlet winked back.

6. A Problem Shared

Hamlet and the ghost had a wonderful summer holiday. Every day the ghost went off sightseeing and every night he returned to No. 13 Irving Terrace.

Hamlet didn't see him come and go because he was asleep whenever the ghost set off and returned again.

The pair of them had a set routine. Each evening Hamlet would go to bed in the normal way and fall asleep. At midnight Hamlet would wake up, go to the cupboard and find the friendly ghost waiting for him there. After about an hour of conversation the ghost would yawn and say, 'I'm afraid it's time for bed. I don't know about you, Hamlet, but I need my beauty sleep.' And Hamlet would say goodnight to the ghost, close the cupboard door, get back into bed and go to sleep.

In the morning Hamlet always looked inside the cupboard the moment he woke up, but however early it was the ghost had always gone.

As well as being very friendly and very polite, the ghost was also very punctual. When Hamlet opened the cupboard door on the stroke of midnight, the ghost was always there — except once. One Saturday night, about three weeks into the holidays, the ghost failed to appear. There was no sudden banging sound at midnight, so Hamlet didn't wake up until six in the morning — when he rushed to the cupboard and found nobody there.

The next night everything was back to normal. At midnight Hamlet heard a sudden noise that woke him up with a start. He nipped out of bed, ran to the cupboard and found his friend sitting on the rug as usual.

'I'm frightfully sorry about last night,' said the ghost apologetically.

'That's all right,' said Hamlet. 'Where were you?'

'At Hampton Court,' said the ghost. 'And guess who I bumped into? The Queen of England!'

'Really!' said Hamlet, who was very impressed.

'Well, two Queens of England actually. They'd both been wives of your King Henry the Eighth. They've been dead for years, of course, but they were fascinating to talk to. We nattered away for hours and before I knew it the clock was striking midnight and it was too late to get home. They were very sweet and invited me to spend the night at Hampton Court. I really couldn't refuse.'

'Of course not,' said Hamlet.

'They've got a very grand place there you know,' said the ghost, 'but I must say I prefer it here at Irving Terrace. It's a lot smaller, of course, but it's *much* cosier. I told them all about you.'

Hamlet was very pleased to think that two of the wives of King Henry the Eighth had been talking about him, Hamlet Brown, a very ordinary nine-year-old schoolboy from Hammersmith, West London.

'They said you must look in on them sometime,' continued the ghost.

'I'll do my best,' said Hamlet, thinking to himself that it wouldn't be easy to persuade his parents to take him to Hampton Court to visit the ghosts of a couple of queens who had been dead for five hundred years!

Since that first Sunday morning when Susan had told her mother that she thought her brother was going round the bend, Hamlet hadn't said anything about ghosts to anyone. He had decided to keep his visitor a secret.

Susan sometimes teased him at breakfast saying, 'Met any good ghosts lately?' but on the whole she left him alone. She was too busy working on her project. She had put together over forty very large pages of facts and figures and drawings and pictures all about the human body. She was sure this was going to be the best project she had ever done.

Hamlet, needless to say, hadn't started on his project at all. The holiday was half gone now and he was beginning to get anxious. One night – it was the night after the ghost had spent a second day at the Tower of London visiting another of King Henry the Eighth's wives – Hamlet decided to share his worries with his friend.

'I don't know what to do,' said Hamlet. 'We're supposed to hand the project in on the first day of term. Susan's almost finished hers and I haven't even started mine.'

'What's yours about?' asked the ghost.

'I don't know. I can't think of anything. Susan suggested dinosaurs, but I don't know anything about dinosaurs. I don't know anything about *anything*!'

'Nonsense,' said the ghost. 'You know lots about lots of things.'

'Such as?'

'Ghosts,' said the ghost. 'Why don't you make your project all about ghosts?'

'That's a brilliant idea,' said Hamlet. And it was.

7. The Ghost Writers

Night after night, from midnight to one o'clock, the light burned bright in the bedroom of Hamlet Brown at No. 13 Irving Terrace as the nine-year-old schoolboy and the five-hundred-year-old ghost worked away at Hamlet's project.

When they had finished it was without doubt the biggest and best project on ghosts the world had ever seen. It contained absolutely everything anyone could ever want to know about ghosts and ghouls and things that go bump in the night. There were the names and addresses of all the most famous haunted castles in the country. There was a

complete list of all the most important ghosts in history. There were even drawings of the ghosts of three of the wives of King Henry the Eighth.

'It's fantastic!' said Hamlet when they had finished.

'It's spooktacular!' said the ghost with a chuckle.

Hamlet was thrilled to have finished his project, but he was sad too, because as they came to the end of their work on the project they came to the end of the holiday as well.

On the very last night of the holiday Hamlet told the ghost he'd got a surprise for him.

'Oh good,' said the ghost. 'I love surprises. What is it?'

'It's a midnight feast,' said Hamlet.

'That sounds fun, but where are we going to have it?' asked the ghost.

'In the kitchen.'

'Where's that?'

'Downstairs,' said Hamlet. 'I'll show you the way.'

'Isn't it a bit risky going downstairs?' asked the ghost, sounding rather nervous.

'Oh no, everyone's fast asleep. Come on, follow me.'

Hamlet led the way and the ghost tiptoed after him out of the bedroom, on to the landing and down the stairs.

When they passed an open door on the first floor, Hamlet whispered to the ghost, 'That's my parents' room. Do you want to see them?'

'No thanks,' whispered the ghost.

'Oh go on,' said Hamlet, putting his head around the door of his parents' bedroom. The ghost put his head around the door too. In the very dim light they could just about make out the shape of Mr Brown lying under the bedclothes next to Mrs Brown who was flat on her back wearing her earplugs and her eyeshade and snoring very gently.

'From what I can see of them they look very nice,' said the ghost as the two friends carried on down the stairs.

'They're not too bad,' said Hamlet.

When they got to the kitchen Hamlet opened the fridge door and asked the ghost what he'd like to have for his feast.

'Well to tell you the truth, Hamlet,' said the ghost, 'I'm not very hungry. I'm not a big eater. None of us ghosts is. But don't let me stop you. I'll just sit and watch while you tuck in.'

So the ghost made himself comfortable in Mr Brown's chair at the head of the kitchen table while Hamlet tucked into jelly and ice-cream.

When Hamlet had finished eating the ghost yawned and said, 'Well, Hamlet, I think it's time for bed. I need my beauty sleep, and you've got a very busy day ahead.'

'So have you,' said Hamlet, who knew that by the time he got to school in the morning the ghost would be back on duty at Elsinore Castle.

'We've had a lot of fun, haven't we?' said the ghost.

Hamlet didn't say anything. He was feeling too sad. For a minute or two the two friends sat in silence at the kitchen table knowing that the time had come to say goodbye but not knowing quite how to say it.

Eventually Hamlet said, 'Can I ask you a favour?'

'Anything you like,' said the ghost.
'Anything — I promise.'

'Would you come and meet my sister? You see, she doesn't believe in ghosts and —'

'I wouldn't want to frighten her,' said the ghost.

'But come and say hello and then she'll know you really exist.'

The ghost wasn't sure that this was a good idea, but he had made a promise and he thought he'd better keep it. So Hamlet and the ghost climbed the stairs and made their way quietly into Susan's room.

Susan was fast asleep, and the two friends crept towards her bed. Hamlet switched on her bedside light and gently tapped his sister on the shoulder. The ghost stood behind him.

'Susan, Susan,' he whispered, 'I've got someone here I'd like you to meet ...'

Susan opened her eyes very wide in the bright light and screamed very loudly!

Hamlet turned round, but there was nobody there — just the sound of footsteps on the landing.

Bleary-eyed and dressed in his pyjamas, Mr Brown appeared at the bedroom door. 'What is it?' he asked.

'I've seen a ghost!' yelled Susan, and she jumped into her father's arms.

8. 'That's the Spirit!'

By breakfast time Susan had recovered from her shock. In fact she was feeling completely better and had decided that what she had seen in the middle of the night wasn't a ghost at all. 'I woke up in the middle of a bad dream,' she said, 'that's all.'

Hamlet didn't say anything, but carried on eating his breakfast and wondered what his teacher would think of his project.

When the Brown children got to school the first thing that each of them did was hand in their projects. You won't be surprised to hear that Susan was awarded the prize for the best project in her class. And it will be no surprise to you either to learn that Hamlet was awarded the prize for the best project in his class as well.

Indeed Hamlet's teacher thought that Hamlet's project was so excellent that she showed it to Mrs Norgate, who was so impressed by it that she told the whole school at assembly that 'Hamlet Brown's project on ghosts is the best project I have come across in over thirty years of teaching.' Everybody clapped Hamlet, who went bright red but felt very pleased at the same time.

When Susan and Hamlet got home to No. 13 Irving Terrace they reported the good news to their parents, who were delighted to have two such clever children.

'I think they deserve a treat, don't you?' said Mrs Brown to her husband.

'Methinks they do indeed!' said Mr Brown.

'How about a trip to the fun fair — it's back on Ealing Common on Saturday.'

'Oh yes,' said Hamlet.

'All right,' said Susan. 'But I'm not going on the ghost train whatever happens.'

'Oh I am,' said Hamlet.

'And so am I,' said Mr Brown.

'I think ghost trains are silly,' said Susan, 'and I don't believe in ghosts anyway.'

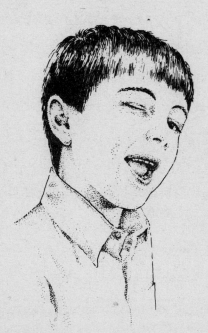

'Well, I *do*,' said Hamlet firmly.

'That's the spirit!' said Mr Brown, with a chuckle. And he winked at Hamlet, who looked a little surprised and then grinned from ear to ear and winked back.

'Yes,' said Hamlet, 'that's the spirit!'